LAURENT GRAFF

Laurent Graff was born in 1968.

His other books include:

Il est des nôtres, 2000
Les Jours heureux, 2001
La Vie sur Mars 2003
Voyage, voyages 2005
Il ne vous reste qu'une photo à prendre 2007
Selon toute vraisemblance 2010

THE SCREAM

This book is supported by the Institut Français as part of the Burgess Programme.

First published in the UK in 2012 by Aurora Metro Books
67 Grove Avenue, Twickenham, TW1 4HX
www.aurorametro.com   info@aurorametro.com

The Scream English translation © 2012 Cheryl Robson and Claire Alejo
Le Cri © le dilettante 2006
Reproduced in English by permission of ÉDITIONS LE DILETTANTE, 19, rue Racine, 75006 Paris, France

With thanks to: Laurane Marchive, Lesley Mackay, Neil Gregory, Martin Gilbert, Simon Smith, Jack Timney, Richard Turk, Candida Cruz, Alex Chambers and Ziallo Gogui
10 9 8 7 6 5 4 3 2 1
All rights are strictly reserved
For rights enquiries contact info@aurorametro.com

No part of this publication may be reproduced, stored in or introduced into a retrieval system, or transmitted in any form, or by any means (electronic, mechanical, photocopying, recording or otherwise without the prior permission of the publisher. Any person who does any unauthorised act in relation to this publication may be liable to criminal prosecution and civil claims for damages.

In accordance with Section 78 of the Copyright, Designs and Patents Act 1988, the author asserts his moral right to be identified as the author of the above work.

This paperback is sold subject to the condition that it shall not, by way of trade or otherwise, be lent, resold, hired out, or otherwise circulated without the publisher's prior consent in any form of binding or cover other than that in which it is published and without a similar condition being imposed on the subsequent purchaser.

Printed by Good News Digital Books, UK
ISBN: 978-1-906582-25-8

THE SCREAM

LAURENT GRAFF

Translated by
Cheryl Robson and Claire Alejo

AURORA METRO BOOKS

To Mia

'With the coming of Dean Moriarty began the part of my life you could call my life on the road.'

On the Road, Jack Kerouac

'*Alors si tu croises un enfant qui demande*
Où va tout le blanc quand la neige fond?
Dis-lui que ça fait gonfler les torrents
Que ça fait souffler le vent
Pour emporter plus loin
Trop loin tous les gens.'

Le vent décime, Renaud Papillon Paravel

ONE

There are less and less cars. Yesterday, I clocked four hundred customers. They can hardly be bothered to wind down the window to pay. They frown at you, or look annoyed. They leave without a word — not even a thank you, no goodbye. I know the toll booth's not the best place to chat but it's the least you'd expect.

I've been working for seven days on the trot. Usually, I do a three or four day shift, no more. We're short-staffed; people don't turn up. I've tried to reach Calo several times but he doesn't pick up. He hasn't been in since Monday.

Today, there are just two of us on the entire toll station, only two counters open. Luckily, there are some automated coin machines and ones that take plastic payment cards too. But if you need to go and take a piss, it's really inconvenient. Mind you, considering the flow of traffic right now, one counter would probably do.

I'm not complaining. The truth is I like my job. Here in my toll booth, in the midst of it all, watching the constant stream of vehicles, I feel like I'm sitting in a privileged place. I've got a front row seat at a show. And the highway is demonstrating its special knowledge, like an endless print-out tracing each single journey. The volume of traffic varies, from the hectic pace of weekends to the slowness of midweek, from the early morning rush to late night serenity; the highway follows the pace of life. And I have the advantage of a spectacular view.

I've come across millions of faces. Some I remember, like markers on the way. The whole of humanity has filed past me, framed by an open window or a lifted visor. People say 'hello' to me hundreds of times a day, thousands of hands reach out towards me with a fee. I've been thanked in every language. Who else has a claim to such a grand overview of the world?

I listen to the radio. Just for background noise. I've finally discovered a station that doesn't give out its name, just broadcasts music non-stop; hits from the 1940s, Bing Crosby, Frank Sinatra, Nat King Cole. It's nice. A voice introduces the songs. Some stations have stopped broadcasting completely. People don't listen to the radio any more.

I feel sorry for Calo. In the last fifteen years, he's the only colleague I've ever really got on with. Before he came to work for the Highway Authority, he used to work for the Department of Transport but he got fired for stealing traffic signs. He's been mad about traffic signs since he was a kid. By the age of ten he knew the Highway Code off by heart. He started out collecting model traffic signs, arranging them carefully in a glass display cabinet. To extend his collection, he'd use cardboard or balsa wood to make them himself, from the everyday to the rarest, from the universal **No Entry** to the Australian Highways' **Kangaroos Crossing**. Sometimes, he'd even turn his hand to creating new signs, such as:

Danger Risk of Homeless People

or

Female Only Underground Car Park

For his fifteenth birthday, he was given a real sign – **No Overtaking** – which his father had surreptitiously lifted in the middle of the night. Then, following his father's example (which he soon regretted), he started going out at night armed with a wrench, secretly bringing stolen signs back into the house, and hiding them under his bed.

His mother often asked where this fascination came from. Calo tried to explain how beautiful traffic signs were to him, their simple, self-evident appeal. How their pure symbolic power gave them undeniable authority. He could go on forever on the subject. The **No Entry** sign was by far his favourite. For him it was the ultimate sign, an icon, the Marilyn Monroe of the roadside, a sign that had everything:

"Look at the minimalism, the perfection! A white line on a red background inside a circle: there's nothing to beat it!"

Collections – they're strange things, aren't they? When I was six or seven years old, I used to collect dust-bunnies. Dust-bunnies are those little bundles of fluff that form along skirting boards or under the furniture. I used to store them in special little handmade boxes. When she cleaned the house, my mother kept them for me. There are loads of kinds of dust-bunnies, made up of all sorts of materials depending on whereabouts they form.

I don't really hang out with the other staff. There's a big turnover; people move around a lot, from one toll gate to another, between the main railway station and all the different exits in the area. Whereas I asked to stay put at this toll station; they agreed to let me. Some of my colleagues prefer to work at the smaller exits, where it's quieter. But I hear some of those exits have been shut down now, due to a lack of staff. People have to go further along the highway to get off now.

There was a guy who came through earlier on today, holding his head in his hands. He was moaning, obviously in pain. He had trouble handing me the money, because he was curled up in his seat, in agony. I passed him his change but he dropped the coins on the road next to his car. He didn't bother picking them up. Just drove off calmly and then suddenly took off. I watched hopelessly, as he faded away in the distance.

*

The cashier who was working next to me yesterday didn't show up this morning. Apart from the automated gates, the tolls are all shut going the other way, inland; there's no-one working. At the moment, it seems to be all right. I haven't seen any drivers stuck, nobody's complained. Let's hope it goes on like that. And, the fact is, the amount of traffic is steadily decreasing. I've only clocked about fifty cars so far today. The faces grow more and more contorted. One woman was literally crying out in pain. When I opened the barrier, she screamed out desperately:

"Help me! I beg you! It's unbearable!"

And then she carried on.

When I went into the office, I caught sight of the technician who maintains the automated coin machines. I noticed a highway services vehicle cruise by as well, probably on patrol. There are still a few employees left on the highway.

But when I picked up my till this morning, I noticed that yesterday's takings hadn't been touched. Every evening, I count the cash, to work out the total for the day then I leave the money in the office in a little pouch with my account number. Today, I found everything just as I'd left it, in exactly the same place. Nobody has been in to collect the funds.

When Calo started working for the State Highways

Authority, he made sure the management didn't find out why he got fired from the Transport Department. If they'd known about him stealing those signs, they'd never have trusted him with a cash till. And they do check thoroughly into people's backgrounds! I don't know how he pulled it off, but he managed it.

I've always worked here at the toll station. I applied for a job that I saw advertised by the Highways Authority, and I managed to pass all the tests. But I didn't end up here purely by chance. When we used to go on holiday in the summer (me and my parents that is), I was always fascinated by the long tarmac river that swept the drivers along, the smooth, unvarying surface that rolled on to infinity under our wheels. The highway seemed to offer an unreal world, surrounded by countryside – something fantastical – like a theme park, perfectly organised, with rest areas, entertainments, restaurants, services and tolls. Entering it was fun, like a game, where you kept within a few simple rules, following the colour coded signs along the way.

At lunch we'd stop and have a picnic on wooden benches among other players. Each person could play along at his or her own pace. At the end of the day, we'd wearily turn off the highway, with the feeling of having won.

When I tell my workmates that I like my job and I'm happy doing it, they smirk a bit. They drone on about how fed up they are with this bloody shit job. I avoid them. I don't join in their conversations. At the end of the day, I'm no worse off, right now, here on my own.

This afternoon, a female driver stopped, looking embarrassed:

"I'm sorry, I haven't got any money left. Impossible to get any out of the bank. And on top of that, it took my card so I can't pay you."

Not only was she upset, but she looked strained, exhausted from hours of mental anguish.

"What can you do?" she asked.

Her name was Joras. We filled out an exception form in triplicate. Usually, you only do this for special cases – official cars, military convoys, important guests, that kind of thing. I gave her one copy and I kept the other two. She thanked me with a smile and I lifted the barrier. She waved back at me in a friendly way and then drove off. She works in an office, not far from here.

*

THE SCREAM

Calo is on the living-room floor, stretched out. He's gripping his head in both hands, his mouth is gaping, his eyes are bulging, frozen in horror, fixed on the ceiling. Road signs of every conceivable kind cover every inch of the walls; others are scattered around the room. In his agony, Calo must have knocked some signs over and spread them around the floor. His body is lying between a **Slippery Surface** and a **No Parking** sign. All roads meet here. Each sign is a portal to a different road like a key opening a door. Any moment you expect to see some ethereal vehicle appear, some ghostly pedestrian crossing over. You can almost hear the faint hum of traffic, an ambulance siren somewhere in the distance, the chug of a heavy vehicle, the fleeting roar of a motorbike. Inside these walls there's a world frozen like Pompeii, echoing with the last vestiges of a vanished civilisation whose signposts are all that remain. In his pain, contorted like a torture victim, Calo looks like an icon, the very image of Man plagued with suffering and death.

*

Two cars and a motorbike went past. The first driver stopped just before the barrier, almost smashed into it. I haven't seen that maintenance technician again and as for the motorbike cops, attached to the toll station to step in if there's a problem, they seem to have deserted the place several days ago. I'd have been really cross if he'd damaged the barrier. The man had to get out of his car to come over to my cabin and pay for his ticket. He staggered over, shaking with terrible convulsions, and when he opened his mouth, a long hoarse rattling sound escaped. As for the motorbike driver, he didn't even bother to lift up the visor of his helmet. His head was thrown back as if he'd just taken a powerful blow to the chin and his hands looked painfully deformed despite his leather gloves. Apart from those three customers, nobody else has come past since this morning.

There's a standard daily programme on the radio. I didn't notice it at first but then when I was unwrapping my sandwich at half-past twelve, and Nat King Cole's *Blue and Sentimental*, started playing, a feeling of *déjà vu* stopped me in my tracks. The day before, I'd done exactly the same thing at exactly the same time accompanied by exactly the same music. Far from putting me off my lunch, it made me smile a bit, and I tucked into my ham sandwich with relish. I'll even be able to go without a watch soon, with the mellow tones of those old crooners to go by.

I had a brief chat with a cop who was on

his way to take up a post in the Vroult valley. He's all alone, like me, guarding the highway.

"There's not a great deal to watch, but never mind!"

So he set up his radar trap on the side of the road anyway, and sat in his special patrol car, waiting, just in case. The occasional driver who makes use of the highway now, tends to crawl along. Yesterday, he did manage to clock one driver who was speeding; he was doing 150 kph instead of 130 kph. He was the only one though.

"It's funny, you're stuck on the same programme as me," he said.

Now he's alone, he has the freedom to listen to music; no-one's going to call him on his radio. But he keeps his walkie-talkie next to him just in case, you never know.

"I love this one! '*Cheek to cheek.*'"

He turned up the volume and started swaying gently, his eyes half-closed with a little dreamy smile.

"'*Heaven, I'm in heaven... dancing cheek to cheek.*'"

He considered the sky through his windscreen, "Oh hell! It looks like there's a load of rain on the way. I'm gonna pack up my radar before it starts tipping down. See you again! I won't be far away."

Long purple streaks began to cut across the sky.

*

I can't stop replaying the image of Calo in his living-room. The faces of the dead stay in your mind forever. The first time I saw a corpse, I was fifteen. It was a friend the same age as me. A car had knocked him down outside the gates of my high school. I wasn't a witness to the accident, but I went to the funeral home. To see. You have to really see death to believe in it. I examined his face – cold, empty, hard, exactly what it ought to be – the face of death, that's how it is! Dead people smiling, that's pure fantasy! Death makes a point of erasing every trace of life, so there's no confusion. *Previously, during life, everything was possible; now, it's death's turn, it's over; no more larking about.* That's why the best actor will always be a bad corpse. I waited to be all alone with my friend's body and then I brought my hand up to his face. I touched his cheek very carefully just to see what it felt like. It was like touching a great glacial void.

A heavy downpour came and went. The rain washed the road surface clean within minutes. The highway resembles an expanse of sea where rare amphibious vehicles float, ghost ships gone adrift.

THE SCREAM

Yesterday's female driver, Joras, showed up again with the same issue. We greeted one another with a friendly "hello". We filled out another exception form.

"I'm really sorry. But I'm afraid we're going to have to resort to this process quite often."

She goes to the hospital every day. One evening, right below the very windows of her office, there was an accident at the traffic lights. The junction is known to be dangerous and there are frequent accidents. Alerted by the sirens, she looked out of the window. Though she noticed the car straight away, she thought it was just the same model, nothing more. Then she noticed the second vehicle involved in the accident and it was too strong a coincidence for it not to be real – as absurd and improbable as it seemed. Right under her window, her husband and her lover had collided. Could it have turned out any other way? Thrown together by a chance meeting at a crossroads, they were too close for just a single moment. Could they have passed by without realising and avoided the crash? Maybe, if they hadn't noticed. Maybe there were other times when they'd passed each other, without realising, and it had all gone smoothly. But, on that particular evening, in that particular place, under the eyes of the woman who secretly linked them both – tragedy prevailed. The question is: Without this link, would the accident have happened? And that's the question Joras keeps asking herself as she visits each of the two men in the hospital.

It's deserted now, the hospital. There's only one nurse left to take care of the last two patients – Joras' husband and her lover. They both lay there in a deep coma, in adjoining cubicles. Joras moves from one to the other, keeping the father of her children company and then the man who makes her dream.

She feels guilty. After all, she's a loose woman. Chance had nothing to do with it. She's sure of that. The nurse explained to her that they both needed her support, that her presence was vital. People in a coma can feel when a loved one is close by. So, she sits and holds hands with them – the right hand for her husband and the left hand for her lover.

Which hand should she hold tighter? She feels torn that she can't help them both with the same conviction. With the necessary degree of honesty and fairness. Inevitably, it's a competition. She's that junction where they both collided. She has to let one go first.

Memories come rushing back during this hand holding time. Each memory is weighed on the scale that measures the life expectancy of the two men. A smile escapes from her lips, but she smothers it straight away, afraid of showing more favour to one than the other. On her way back from the hospital, she calculates how much love she has given to each of them. Did she really love each man equally?

*

For the entire morning, not a single driver came by so I ducked out for two minutes to take a piss and coming out of the toilets, what do I see? A van parked up right in front of my toll gate. Bloody hell!

A dodgy-looking guy with a shaved head and tattoos all over his arms was behind the wheel. Sitting next to him, a black girl in a leopard print mini-skirt and a crop top was filing her nails.

"We've been here for ten minutes! What the fuck were you playing at?"

I apologised. The guy handed me a hundred euro note.

"Don't you have any change?" I asked.

"No, I've only got big notes. Are you gonna let us through or what? Give me a break, will you! Nobody cares about this shit, man! Come on!"

The black girl gave me a big smile, all sparkly. While most of her co-workers prefer to use another name for work, she'd always kept her real name – Grace. She'd come over from Cameroon three years ago and started out on the street, turning tricks for a pimp, a nice old guy by the name of Gilbert. He'd invented the whole vans thing; he came up with the idea. Since they'd made it illegal to walk the streets and as brothels were no longer permitted either, why not fit out a vehicle, like a transit van (he'd driven a mobile library when he was young), that would park up in a certain place? With a girl sat ostensibly behind the wheel, it was possible to pick up clients and operate in pretty basic conditions that were absolutely legal. It was a big success – then everybody started doing it. As the instigator of the 'van thing', Gilbert tried to claim the right to exclusivity but it cost him his life. Grace was passed on to a nasty young pimp called Rachid. Sometimes he'd push her around a bit, but so far, it wasn't too bad.

"Eh, Rachid, ask him if he knows anywhere!"

They were looking for a busy spot to park the van up. They thought the highway might be a good place.

"You know, there aren't that many drivers on the road anymore."

THE SCREAM

Rachid looked long and hard at the road ahead of him.

"Don't worry, we'll find a place, one way or another."

The young pimp wound the window up, shutting out the sight of Grace's dazzling smile.

To keep myself busy, I do crosswords. I'm not really bored, but sitting around doing nothing isn't easy. I wanted to buy myself a new puzzle book in the service station at St Jean but there was no-one behind the counter. I picked one up anyway and left three euros next to the till. As I was leaving the shop, I passed a maintenance man sweeping the car park. Waving my puzzle book, I called out:

"I've left the money next to the checkout."

He nodded back "okay". Usually, I only do crosswords when I'm on holiday. What's got seven letters and means: *torment?*

At the end of the toll station, there's a poster for Road Safety that reads: "I'm holding on for life!" And it shows two hands gripping a steering wheel set against a floral landscape. After a rather dramatic period when there were a lot of shocking posters, all the advertising campaigns are now like this one – upbeat in tone and resolutely optimistic.

It's over. The last driver came past earlier

today. In a dreadful state – his eyes staring horribly, a scream bursting from his lips, his face distorted, his body crushed. I wondered how he could possibly still be driving.

Daniel, the cop, dropped by for a chat in the afternoon. '*You made me so happy sometimes, You made me feel so sad, I didn't want to tell you. You made me love you...*' He left his radar on the hard shoulder, like a fisherman leaves his fishing line dangling whilst going for a stroll.

He stopped in at the service station to buy something to eat.

"You want some crisps? You know, we should make the effort to go to the restaurant at the Services in *La Croix*. They'll feed us up down there, you can bet on it. Why don't we make a little trip, one of these days?"

I'm still reluctant to leave the toll booth. I usually bring a sandwich for lunch. And someone might come along when I'm not there. What's more, it's where I belong. I feel fine here. Even if nobody drives by anymore, even if there are no more fish out there, I like to sit and wait beside the river.

"Maybe later, all right?"

"Okay if you like."

Joras was distraught. She didn't say one word. She

simply picked up her copy of the exception form and nodded her head to say goodbye. Today, she thought she'd felt a sign of life in the hand she was holding, a little quiver. Her eyes sprang to the face immediately, looking for any trace of movement behind the eyelids, the hint of a smile, anything that might point to someone coming back to life. Then, she suddenly crossed to the other bed to see whether similar signs of life were occurring there. But as she examined each of the faces, neither showed any sign of movement, both remained frozen in a deep sleep. How long would this torture last? Increasingly, she felt as if it all depended on her, as if she was the only one capable of bringing this torment to an end. She had the power in her hands through the pressure she exerted, to give the green light for life to return.

It was her husband who'd gone through the red light at this damned intersection, the one who'd caused the fatal collision. But in his case, the mistake was almost understandable – it was hard to blame him. As for her lover, he'd paid for his recklessness too. Now she was completely worn out with the stress of it all – too exhausted to take it any longer. How could she possibly untangle the terrible knot created by the crossing of those two paths?

On the morning of the 22nd of August, two thieves made off with *The Scream* and *The Madonna* by Edvard Munch from the Oslo City Museum. After threatening both the guards and visitors with their guns, the thieves felt they had a right to take possession of the famous Norwegian painter's two masterpieces. In their hurried escape, they dropped the paintings several times, raising concerns about damage. To this day, neither the criminals nor the paintings have been located.

The Scream depicts a man on a coastal path,

next to a railing that divides the painting into two; the sun is setting and long wisps of blood-coloured clouds snake across the sky. In the foreground, the central character, his features distorted due to some indescribable pain, opens his mouth to scream while protecting his ears with both hands. Is he the one forcing out a mighty scream? Or is he the victim of some kind of extraordinary, unbearable howling that fills the picture? In the background, the two passers-by don't seem to hear anything. They just carry on walking, unperturbed, in the twilight.

From a long way off, I make out the shapes of two pedestrians. They're walking along the roadway. A boy and a girl. They're carrying backpacks and surfboards under their arms. They're moving along at a steady pace, without seeming in the least bit tired. They stroll along, one after the other, without talking. When they reach the toll station, they hang about for a while and decide to stop. They go over to the office, which has a small lawn, a bit of green space around it. They put down their bags and look to settle there. The grass looks a bit scruffy as it hasn't been mown for weeks, but the place seems to suit them.

Then the boy starts flattening a patch of grass

THE SCREAM

to pitch a tent. He tramples the grass, stamping it down as if he's putting out a fire. Meanwhile, the girl unfolds the tent canvas, rubbing at some dirty marks. I watch them from my booth; they haven't noticed me yet. They set themselves up there, fixing their little shelter steadily with stakes that they bang into the ground with stones. Then they leave their backpacks to go and take a look around. Actually, it's a pretty good choice as they've got all the facilities they need here – toilets, showers, drinking water and even a microwave in the office. They make themselves at home, rummaging around and bringing various objects they've found, back to their camp. I'm reluctant to get involved. I just let them get on with it. After all, it's not my problem. I'm only here to take the tolls. I just hope they're not planning to stay too long.

As usual these days, Daniel dropped by for a chat before positioning himself down the road in his car to watch the highway. *'On the sunny side of the street.'* He doesn't bother to set up his radar anymore, he just sits in his vehicle and keeps an eye on the deserted highway stretching out before him. I told him about the two campers.

"Oh yes! I saw them, yesterday. A boy and a girl with surfboards. Hitch-hikers. They aren't doing any harm, they're just young," he said.

And then he launched into tales of his teenage adventures on the open road, with a rucksack on his back and no cares in the world.

"Those were the days!"

I haven't travelled much in my life. The truth is – I've never been on a plane. When I was with my parents, we went on holiday in this country, never went abroad. Later on, I never felt any desire to go much further. Either you go around the world – or you stay and watch it go around. But in the end, you see the same thing. I tend to think that travelling requires a lot of energy and an incredible commitment to maintain a few captivating delusions. I don't have a thirst for new horizons, a crazy appetite for foreign lands, or the need for a change of scenery. Even when the landscape changes, in reality, you haven't moved. Wherever you go, you always follow the same road. The one that carries you along.

As a child, I heard of lot of tales about the various travels of one of my uncles; he was one of those legendary figures who creates some kind of mystique in the family circle, feeding conversations:

"You know where he is at the moment? – Last time we heard, he was in India. He sent us a postcard."

Everybody travelled along with him, vicariously. Back then, I wanted to be like him too, to earn some respect and inspire some dreams at family reunions. I'd always imagined that, in turn, I'd be talked about with the same fascination, the same silent admiration as my uncle. But as the years went by, I set my sights a little lower, to a point where I was happy just to accept things as they are. And the uncle? He spent his last days in an old people's home where nobody ever visited him.

The two campers have noticed me in my booth. But once they realised I wasn't going to do anything about them, they ignored me. They just laid down on the grass beside their tent to take in the sun. Despite there being a hundred metres between us I can hear them laughing and chatting. It provides me with a little entertainment. Having said that, boredom has never been a problem for me. I like being bored. I see it as a natural part of everyday life, a mild climate for the soul, like being in a hammock suspended in time between two palm trees. Boredom and the highway fit together perfectly; it's a way of immunising yourself with a gentle monotony, like a thin thread penetrating the mind's eye, easing your troubled soul. When people get irritated or impatient, when they make rude gestures, I simply sink back into a bored state of weariness with delight.

At first it was like a very weak signal, a faint whisper you could only just make out. The source of the noise couldn't be identified; it wasn't carried by the air waves and didn't spread like most sounds. It occupied every dimension, radiating equally in every direction without diminishing. It was as if the air you breathe had become resonant, all the way inside your chest.

Initially, people blamed it on a physical affliction, some sort of tinnitus. Whether temporary or permanent, tinnitus causes a disturbing buzzing or whistling in the ear and can be an absolute ordeal for those suffering from it. Treatments: hearing aids and electrical stimulation of the nerves have rather poor results. You have to live with it; there's no other choice.

You saw people constantly touching or massaging their ears, sometimes they'd poke a finger inside to try and fix whatever was going wrong. It didn't help at all; it was still there. Then people tried to protect themselves from the 'noise' by covering up their ears. But whatever they tried, the 'noise' was still there, omnipresent, and against all logic, it never went

THE SCREAM

away. It remained constant, inescapable.

Gradually, as the days went on, it increased in intensity. Measurements showed a logarithmical progression of two decibels per day. The average pain threshold is around a hundred decibels. The 'noise' now resembled a shriek, a scream, a howl. The experience was of hearing something but the origin of that 'something' was so elusive, and its nature so uncertain, that the phenomenon went beyond the auditory. The 'noise' was inside every single thing and inside us too.

Everybody had an explanation. The craziest hypotheses did the rounds. Authorities and scientists lined up to give their interpretations: secret weapon, physical manifestation, plot, alien message, last gasp of the dying earth, advance warning of a great tsunami, God's growing anger, meteors about to strike and so on. The religious sects took up the event as a way of boosting their numbers, adding their prophetic voices to the general cacophony.

However, a few lone individuals, no-one knows how many, showed no reaction whatsoever to the phenomenon. While the entire world was living through a nightmare, wincing with pain and putting their fingers in their ears, here and there, a man or a woman remained perfectly unaffected by the 'noise', untouched, on another wavelength.

*

'It's only a paper moon.' The two campers crawl out of their tent. They stretch up to the sky and check the weather. It looks set to be a sunny day again. They look toward me to check if I'm still there. The boy gives me a kind of nod. And then they decide to go off on an excursion, around the castle of Breal which was signposted on the highway as ten kilometres away. They make a well-known cheese there, very creamy, the Breal. They grab some towels and head towards the showers. The girl has long blond hair that hangs down her back. She follows her partner, with her surfboard under her arm.

Sat in my toll booth, I like to amuse myself by spinning around in my swivel chair. I run at the chair, hop on then close my eyes with my feet in the air, until I stop spinning, like a lottery wheel. The choice of view offered to me doesn't vary a lot, between the highway in one direction or another, and the toll station.

Still I feel as if I'm sitting at a strategic point, on the axis of the whole world. There are some places like that, apparently insignificant, but

THE SCREAM

secretly touching a vital nerve, really special places in the immensity of it all. On the secret map showing all the extraordinary places that are dotted around the universe, I'm sure there must be a dot for my swivel chair.

In the distance you can see oil wells off to one side of the highway. Some kind of machinery, drilling relentlessly into the earth to collect a few litres of the precious black liquid. The sight of those machines, left unattended, always makes me think of a world deserted by man. With their mechanical pumping system and robotic arms, it seems they'll go on forever, even when there's no oil left to collect. Everything else can stop but they'll keep on drilling into the depths of the earth.

I can hear the roar of a car engine but scanning the horizon there's nothing visible. It must be quite a powerful car for its engine to make such a noise. The highway has become unbelievably silent, mute, like a sea without the sound of the crashing waves. I finally catch sight of the car in the distance – it's black. It's a sporty model, perhaps with a soft-top. The car slows down and comes to a halt in front of me – yes, it's a convertible. The driver can't be seen through the tinted windows. Seconds pass but the window doesn't move. I try to imagine the face of the man hidden behind the smoky glass of the cool American car. Finally, the window slides down: Wow, it's Florent Pagny, the singer! With his blond hair and orange glasses. He hands me the exact money in coins and closes the window immediately. Once the barrier goes up, he takes off at full speed with a fabulous *vroo-oom*.

He's not the first celebrity I've seen go through here. Actors, singers, men and women in the public eye – once in a while they slip into the mainstream of traffic on the highway. I'm always taken aback by their unexpected appearance. Thrown off balance by this almost supernatural intrusion, reality flickers momentarily – you need time to adjust. The glimpse you get through the window of the car suddenly merges with the image on the TV screen and smack! There's a huge tear in the fabric of life. That's why this kind of interaction has to be as brief as possible lest the celebrity loses all credibility. Stars have to project this amazing energy and create an image, a fantasy, to protect themselves from reality. One day, I saw a really famous actor driving an ordinary little car, wearing a cheap checked shirt. When he said to me:

"Hello, mate. Thanks very much. Bye," I was

so disappointed!
I actually thought it might be a bad look-alike.

*

Joras stopped by for a bit longer today as she needed to talk:

"You know that book, *Sophie's Choice*? It's the story of a woman who was deported by the nazis to Auschwitz with her two children. As she's entering the camp, just off the train, a German officer orders her to choose between keeping her son or her daughter. Of course, she refuses, she can't choose between them but under pressure from the soldier who's threatening to take both the children, in a state of panic, she makes a choice. Later on she survives, alone. I feel as if I'm in the same position – it's terrible.

"I think I was holding my husband's hand slightly tighter today. Nothing is forcing me to make a choice between them; no-one is threatening to kill either one of them. I'm the one, if I'm honest, who's creating this dilemma, as if it's impossible to save both of them, my husband *and* my lover. There's nothing really stopping me. I could easily support them both equally, with no thought other than their survival – the consequences, that's another story. So what's stopping me?"

Then she looked me in the eye, and asked me straight:

"What if I'm being held back by the sense that I have the power of life and death over them? And the temptation is to use it. I could kill them both, after all. Leave them, abandon them. Just give up."

She left without taking her copy of the exception form. Mind you, we probably don't need to bother with it from now on.

The two campers came back from their excursion towards the end of the day.

*

'The Silent Ones'. A journalist first coined the phrase on television. It was then quickly picked up by others and came to describe all those who weren't sensitive to the 'noise'. Nothing to do with sudden deafness or loss of hearing; it was just a term used to denote something completely inexplicable – the extraordinary difference which saved *"The Silent Ones"*. Another journalist, on another special programme, talked about experiments conducted at the beginning of the 70s as part of the fight against terrorism. Members of the

Baader Meinhof gang or the Red Army faction were allegedly subjected to an experiment, for the purpose of military research, into the effects of sound frequencies on the brain. Locked in an isolation room, the prisoner was subjected to an assault from all kinds of sounds, each one more sophisticated. Most of the time, they would come out in a pitiful state. Then again, there was another journalist, claiming he'd found the source of the catastrophe somewhere deep in the Arctic Circle. Clearly suffering under his extreme weather gear he was pointing to the ice floe that stretched behind him as far as the eye could see.

"It's here! Under the ice!" he screamed into his microphone then began desperately pounding at the ice with a pick. News reports, debates, interviews, programmes – they followed one after another in a frenzy of discussion while speech itself was being threatened with extinction. Then the television fell silent, there were no more journalists and no more special programmes either.

Some of my colleagues, who worked at the quieter tolls on the slip roads (it wasn't possible on the main highway) used to bring a small TV to work to follow the World Cup or the Grand Prix. They'd plug the set in next to them and watch the football or the race on the tiny screen in the time between vehicles. I've never really liked television anyway. I find it difficult to focus, I don't really follow it. I prefer to ignore the screen and look around. Sometimes, instead of watching what's happening on the screen, my attention wanders so that I find myself staring at the thing – the frame, the speakers, even the TV cabinet. When I'm sat on my couch in front of the set, I sometimes feel like I'm a target in the television's sights, so I weave and dodge, like a boxer.

I definitely prefer radio. It doesn't take over – actually it does just the opposite, it lets you daydream as much as you like. Even if the final programme from the last working radio station is a bit repetitive, I never get bored of it. Daniel, the policeman, knows all the songs by heart. He doesn't bother to wear his police cap anymore and he's taken to slicking his hair back the way the crooners used to. The other day, we both went down to the restaurant at the service station at *La Croix* for lunch. I finally agreed to leave my post for a few hours.

Palika, the cook, was all alone in the restaurant. He was serving a single dish of the day and improvising anything else. He acts as the waiter as well now. He was very happy to see us. When we arrived, he was sat at one of the tables in his apron and white hat, waiting for potential customers, while listening to the radio. He jumped up and came over to greet us:

"Welcome! Please take a seat. Smoking or non-smoking? Today's special is: *Blanquette de veau*."

Daniel had the cold meat to start with. I had the tomato salad. Palika apologised for the lack of choice:

"Nobody's coming in any more. I don't want to waste good food. Florent Pagny had lunch here a few days ago. I cooked him trout with almonds. But otherwise, it's been empty. Not a soul."

For dessert, we ordered ice cream. Luckily, the freezers are full of it.

"Coffee's on me!" Palika said.

All in all, we had a nice time and a really good meal. We promised to come back next week and left Palika to his stove.

"Let me know beforehand when you're coming back. I'll do you a nice casserole of braised lamb – you'll rave about it!"

On the way back, we drive past stranded vehicles on the hard shoulder. Lifeless silhouettes, like shop dummies, are the cars' only occupants. Daniel explains to me that he's tried to contact the Emergency Services to have them removed, but nobody's answering. Strangely enough, the drivers seem to have had enough time to pull in and stop on the side of the highway. I can't see any cars that have crashed. As we go up a fairly steep hill, there are several vehicles that seem to have stopped almost one after the other, as if they didn't have the strength to carry on, and gave up in the same place.

I suddenly remember quite an unpleasant thing that I once heard Commander Cousteau say about there being too many people on the earth and that the population would have to be halved for the planet to survive. At the time, I tried to imagine it – half the number of people in the streets, in the shops, on the highway. I mentally eliminated one in every two individuals, at random. Relieved of fifty per cent of its population, the world I imagined took on a different aspect... more fantastical. Life seemed to be light and dreamy, totally unpredictable. Today, with only a few of us left, it's as if somebody's conducting some kind of anthropological experiment. Human life is becoming both simple and meaningful at the same time.

The vegetation is starting to take over again.

THE SCREAM

The verges along the highway have been invaded by long grass while nettles and brambles run rampant. The little hedge that normally grows between the two security barriers has now overgrown it easily on both sides, pushing out long free shoots. Ivy is creeping onto the roadway, like roped climbers on a glacier, digging their crampons into the tarmac.

As we approached the toll station, we saw the two campers, their rucksacks on their backs, about to hit the road again.

THREE

This morning I realised I had a beard. I hadn't noticed it before. A beard like Robinson Crusoe. I thought of a book about a man who decides on a whim to shave off the moustache he's had for a long time. And yet, nobody notices anything – what's more, they tell him he never had a moustache.

Today, Daniel, wasn't wearing his uniform at all but turned up in an amazing white sparkly suit with wide lapels, his hair slicked back as ever. It was quite a surprise to see him driving a police car in that outfit.

"What do you think? Classy, or what? I'm

booking a table at Palika's for lunch tomorrow. Okay with you?"

Joras is back beside her husband and her lover, now both together in the same room. Sitting between the two beds, first she takes hold of the hand on her right, then the one on her left, with her arms crossed:

"I asked the nurse to move them together. I don't like to leave them anymore. I sleep there, I wait by their side. I can't let go of them. I'm their only connection. They hold on to me and together we'll just have to resist the pull of whatever is dragging them away. I had to put all those bad thoughts out of my mind, just focus on their survival. No matter how much they're against each other, I want to take them both by the hand and lead them on from this damned place where they've stopped still. It's ridiculous. The road goes on!"

She clenches her jaw before speaking again:

"In certain places, fatal car accidents were always marked by a cross that was put up by the side of the road. These days, it's more common to see bunches of flowers left along the roadsides, marking the spot on the ground or next to a road sign where a tragedy has occurred. Lives ended there, stupidly.

THE SCREAM

You can believe in fate, and think that's how it is and there's nothing to be done about it. Or you can try to find some kind of meaning in it all. You can laugh or cry about it. And in the end, time heals, the flowers wither, the dead slowly cease to live. Absurd, yes, but there's no other way, you have to keep on going down the road."

Joras looks over to her right, smiling at the face of the man she said 'yes' to twenty years ago, then looks to the left, and smiles at the face of the man who, one day, she didn't say 'no' to. She grips their hands tightly:

"Come on, let's go!"

A tourist bus came by this morning. As well as the driver, there was a passenger sat by the window. He was on a two week trip around the country, visiting all the different places of interest our country prides itself on. It was a lifelong dream he wouldn't have missed for anything in the world. Alone on the bus, he smiled at the landscape flashing past the window.

*

Palika's couscous was divine. To end our meal, we all had a cognac and drank a toast to our enjoyment of the moment. Daniel, in his spangly crooner's outfit, gave us his version of *Star Dust*, using a bottle of fizzy water as a microphone. He's really improved! When we were about to leave, Palika pointed towards a car in the car park. It wasn't there yesterday. He went to take a look: there was no-one inside.

"I'll leave you to it; I'm going to wash up."

Out of curiosity, Daniel and I went over to the vehicle, a high-powered black car with no number plate. The doors weren't locked so Daniel checked inside. He didn't find anything except for a road map in the glove box. Then he opened the boot. There was a big leather portfolio case with shoulder straps inside. Daniel lifted it out and unzipped it.

Inside it was a painting: *The Scream*, by Edvard Munch, 1893. (Tempera on wood, 83.5cm x 66cm.) Munch explained it:

"One evening I was walking along a path, with the town on one side of me and the fjord below. The sun was setting, the clouds were turning blood red. I sensed a scream pass through nature. I had the impression that I'd heard it."

There are four different versions of the painting – the one that Daniel was holding up was the one stolen from the Oslo City Museum several months earlier.

THE SCREAM

"1893! You'd think it was painted yesterday! Look at it!"

The cop handed me the painting; I held it in my hands and stared, mesmerised.

"Hey, what's the matter? Is it this guy here, with the big gob who's bothering you?"

I finally managed to look away from the figure in the painting.

"I'd like to keep it. Do you mind?"

Daniel shrugged, as if to say: "You know, at this point…!"

I put the painting back in its case and carried it back to my toll booth. Once alone, I took it out again and put it down on the floor, leaning it up against the wall so that my eyes could drink it in.

I contemplate it, observe it, examine it. I look at it from my swivel chair; I go closer, squatting, kneeling; I touch it gently, with my fingertips; I follow the sinuous lines of the sky, the bluish waves in the fjord, the diagonal axis of the railings, the outlines of the figure in black, its hands hanging limp, its mouth stretched open wide as if to give birth. I stand up, I sit down again. Never in my life have I ever painted; I've never been interested in art; yet, I feel strangely like a painter in front of this picture, I marvel at the brush work, the intelligence. I understand every detail, every colour: I would have done the same thing. At first sight, I felt a strong connection, I identified with it straight away. Do I have a need to find my own expression in this painting, or is it reflecting what's already within? My eyes constantly go back to it, as if drawn towards a window.

The 'noise' started shortly after the theft of *The Scream* by Edvard Munch from the Oslo City Museum; to be accurate, seven days afterwards. A Norwegian journalist had connected the two events, suggesting the possibility of a mysterious correlation. Over the next few weeks, the image of *The Scream* was used to illustrate the awful pain caused by the 'noise' in an apocalyptic short film. Ivor Stensrud, a man of reason, who was leading the investigation into the theft of the painting, always refused to believe any link between the two, until the moment he was confronted by his own twisted face in the mirror and collapsed onto his bathroom floor. An art dealer from the Ostfold area, to the south-east of the Norwegian capital, was questioned by police before being released for lack of evidence. This man was one of the first known victims of the 'noise'; his body was found a week later in an underground car park. A striking similarity between the facial expression of Munch's central figure and that of the dead art dealer was casually noted down, but little importance was attached to it.

The occupants of the big black sedan abandoned at the restaurant had preferred to get rid of the painting. It was too heavy to carry. The man and woman were from Germany, both experienced dealers in stolen goods. The man, clearly worried, didn't want anything more to do with it.

"I don't like this painting. It's been freaking me out the whole time."

The woman, on the other hand, refused to leave it behind:

"That's absurd! It's only a painting! You can't do that!"

A bit further on, the man stopped the car without warning:

"We change cars. We leave it here, in the boot."

No matter how hard the woman protested, threatening to leave the man if he didn't change his mind, he remained adamant.

"Over fifty million up in smoke! You must be joking? Just because 'his nibs' gets the jitters over a painting!"

The couple left in a small white van with the words *Little Brothers' Building and Renovation Company* on the side.

"Why didn't we keep the car? Look how crappy this van is! I don't believe it!"

Now Munch's masterpiece is in my toll booth; its mute rebellion, its voiceless scream blends into the silence of the highway.

*

I put up a little shelf in my toll booth to sit the painting on, against the window. I didn't want to risk damaging it by fixing it to the wall. The frame Munch used for the painting was quite thick and must have weighed around ten kilos. No wonder the thieves left it behind. I haven't noticed any damage to the canvas though. It's here, right next to me, I just have to stretch out my arm and I can touch it. Sometimes, I even feel like I can hear it.

It's a bit like I've taken in an abandoned animal, or a wounded bird.

Daniel managed to get hold of a white Cadillac to match his suit.

"It was just going to waste, parked up outside a garage; I couldn't leave it."

He took back his gun and the handcuffs, his uniform and the badge. There's nothing left of the cop he used to be: the metamorphosis is complete. Except, he does keep patrolling the highway, stopping at strategic places to check on things. He sings all the old tunes, smiling at himself in his rear-view mirror.

"It looks good like that, your painting. You know what? Maybe the guy is singing. No really, if you look at it in the right way... *'Till the end of time...'* Right, I'm off. See you later!"

It's true. Some singers do cover up one of their ears to carry a tune better. Or they do it to block out an annoying noise somewhere, a slightly over enthusiastic neighbour in a choir, or a crashing cymbal player. But Munch's figure is covering both his ears. Besides, his mouth is wide open, a real pit! If he's singing, he's putting his heart into it! Daniel's remark suggests looking at the picture in a different way, more light-hearted, with more distance. Supposing the figure is singing (I'm willing to give it a try), but I can't help hearing some kind of dirge, a long, mournful and hallucinatory lament. It's hard to imagine anything else. *'Love me tender, Love me do'* doesn't exactly fit in with the background.

I went to the office and picked up a microphone. I put it right next to the figure's mouth to see if it looked right: it's didn't really work. No, he is definitely not singing

Magnificent sunset on the highway, tonight.

I drink it all in, sitting with the flap of my tent open. I've set up a tent right where the two campers had pitched theirs earlier. Of course, the grass had sprung back up since they left so I had to flatten it down again. I just put some of my stuff into a travel bag and decided to set up the tent near the toll station. It's more convenient that way. I'm slowly getting used to the outdoor life and all the little things you need to do; I keep everything organised. In the evening, I take *The Scream* with me; I put it in the tent. I've got everything I need.

When it's all lit up, the toll station towers above me like an enchanted portal; its columns of light an artists' entrance, promising a fabulous spin on a magic roundabout. The gateway creates a separation, a break in time. The toll station becomes a frontier, a passage, a demarcation line. Just as there are remarkable places scattered around the world, there are doorways which unlock the way to the future.

*

I like the simplicity of camping. A canvas cloth stretched between four poles, twisting in the wind, lashed by the heavy rain, is what you call home. The fragility of the shelter; sleeping on the uneven ground; living in cramped conditions and making it your whole universe; possessing nothing, you carry it all in one bag. Being able to pack up and hit the road at any time, sitting there proud but humble in the middle of the vast universe, savouring your insignificance.

I like damp a lot less though. It creeps into everything; it goes through the tent cloth and gets into the clothes, into the sleeping bag, into the food, a real disaster! It's like being at sea! As a precaution, I keep a change of clothes and some food in the office, where it's dry. During the day, I open everything up, leave things to dry out as much as possible. I don't have anything very fancy; it's an old-fashioned orange ridge tent with a zip at the front. You crawl out with aching muscles – 'You – hoo! It's me!' Mind you, I do like my tent. Again, I'm not complaining. It's conceited to moan. When it comes to facial expressions, I prefer to smile. When it comes to screams, I prefer the silent kind.

*

As the 'noise' became more oppressive and frightening, people started hitting the road in a panic, in an insane exodus, in search of a haven of peace. They fled either by themselves, with their families or in organised groups, some going one way, others going the other. How far they travelled didn't make any difference; they were trying to escape their own shadows. Groups of people started drifting along the roadsides, camping here and there. They were all running from their fears, led by an unlikely guide, a new messiah moved by the need to save. But far from weakening, the pain from the 'noise' was intensifying; families fell apart, groups split up as the kilometres passed. Hard shoulders and roadside ditches collected the remains of the unlucky ones, before they disappeared altogether...

I'm a little ashamed to admit it but one day, out of curiosity, I stopped next to one of these camps, at a rest area. There was no-one there; a caravan and a tent had been abandoned. Among the things left lying around, I came across a knife that I liked the look of. I picked it up. It has a curved handle made of varnished wood, reinforced with metal bands and fitted with a very thin, smooth blade. I took it with me. Now, I use it to eat with. It's got some initials engraved on the metal ring: A.G.

Initials hold some kind of suggestive power. Without getting into a mystical rant, it's nevertheless surprising how the association of two letters (in most cases) is able to construe or conjure up a person, whether living or dead. Initials excite the imagination presenting it with an enigma to be solved, but on top of that, initials represent some kind of intimate and mysterious symbol, an authentic artefact of being. A whole hidden, private existence lies in those letters, the abbreviation of a forename and a surname of a being, of a life. A.G. I hold the knife in my hand, as she must have held it, my fingers on her fingers, my sweat on hers. A.G. Who were you? You possessed a knife.

*

In the mornings, I return to my toll booth around nine. Before that, I walk along the toll station, from one end to the other, checking on all the different bays. Nothing has changed since the day before. All the barriers are down; the station is slumbering, silently waiting for the traffic to hypothetically resume. I am the sole guardian, a bit like the attendants at railway crossings (before they became automated) who were responsible for stopping the traffic and lived in a little house between the road and the railway.

When I was a kid, I used to watch one of

those level crossings, during the holidays. We rented a house whose garden and windows looked down on the mainline tracks, as well as the notable house of the railwayman. Shortly before the arrival of the train, the railwayman, who must have been near to retirement, lowered the massive gates using a removable handle. The process required a lot of physical effort and I used to wonder, from my observation post, if he'd manage to close the gates in time. Fortunately, the trains weren't going very fast and the car drivers were fairly patient. Once the road was open to cars again, the railwayman would sit back on his deckchair in the shade and catch his breath. I was around ten years old, and the conscientious way that man worked captivated me; a small cog in the vast mechanism of the world, a traffic controller, a humble switchman. I spent a good deal of that summer glued to the comings and goings at the level crossing.

This morning, standing in the middle of the road, I spent a long time watching the highway stretching out and receding before my eyes, escaping into the distance in the direction of its white painted stripes. The path taken by the central figure in *The Scream* (or is it the path that takes the figure) clearly leads uphill and off to one side, leading the gaze to a vanishing point situated outside the frame, a specific point in the sky above the horizon, the real cyclonic eye of the picture. All the lines lead to it, as if being sucked up and spat out by a deadly whirlpool. Brown streaks create an endless flow on the surface of the path that seems to pour into the sky and nourish it, a kind of irresistible, contradictory current. What is this invisible vanishing point, the source of life and death?

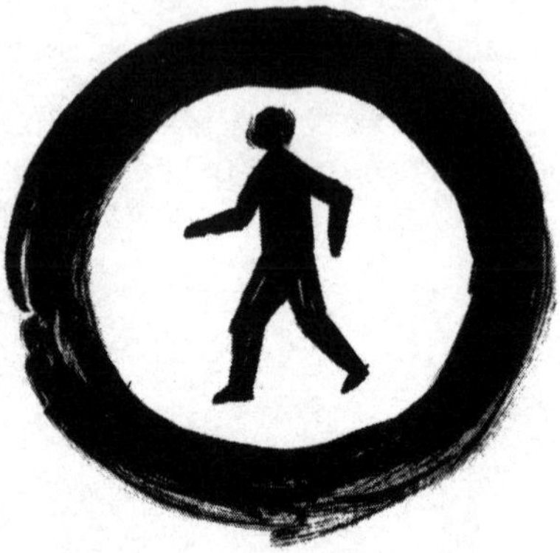

FOUR

There are large brown signs for curiosities, historical sites and interesting things to visit just off the highway: *Breal Chateau, Oil Well, Creux Abbey, Remu Wine Cellars*. They're not there to encourage you to make a detour or get off at the next exit, but more to inform you about the outside world and entertain you with brief descriptions. Then the route becomes more like a guided tour aboard a small train: you turn your head to the right or the left looking for a monument – There it is! *Up there! On the hill!* – or for a place steeped in history – *They say that thousands of men died over there, in those very fields!* – which leads to a little musing on the nature of existence – *whereas nowadays, there are cows grazing there!* The sense of being on some kind of 'guided tour' grows stronger on a bright day, when traffic flows freely and you're feeling relaxed; you can almost forget who's driving – you or the highway? You just let yourself be carried through the countryside, strapped into your seat, on the moving track that is the highway.

On foot, you get all the same feelings, only at a slower pace.

I gave myself permission to leave. I folded my tent, collected my things and placed *The Scream* back in its cover. I faced the road and started walking without turning back, without a single glance back at the toll station.

For the first few metres, you walk; you're the one walking. You move along, one step mechanically following the other. You make small adjustments; you change the position of the bag on your shoulder; you strive for comfort, ease. You go forth into the wide blue yonder. Then, gradually, you distance yourself from the actual walking; with every stride, you become more removed. You build up a momentum, create a rhythm, like a passenger your steps carry you on. *You are now being walked* and the road is *leading you*. It takes over, transports you, carries you on its back. It's blissful to simply let yourself go. From above, you look down on yourself walking.

Land all around me. Like a blind man, I follow the short white stripes, which run like a seam down the road towards the horizon. Little by little, I move on in what seems like dream time, as though the hand is inching forward in some universal clock.

*

I go past Palika's restaurant. Daniel's Cadillac was there in the car park but I didn't stop. The cop will find the toll station deserted, empty. The patch of lawn near the office will be bare too, no more tent. Before leaving, I thought to raise one of the barriers.

I reach the turn off for the hospital. Joras is there by the bedside of the injured, faithfully giving them an emotional transfusion. She doesn't let go; she holds on tight, resisting the pull of the current, fighting tiredness, hopelessness and boredom. You can see her from the corridor, with her arms crossed, split in two yet still devoted, blocking it all out.

I continued on my way, straight on towards infinity.

If my load wasn't so uncomfortable, I'd carry on no problem. I've got my bag with the tent tied to it on one side and *The Scream* hangs in its case on the other. From time to time I take a rest and relax my shoulders. I don't really stop though; I keep hopping like a jogger, waiting for the light to turn red so they can cross. Although I put down my bags and take in the surroundings, the rolling sensation stays with me, like a gentle rocking motion. And then I'm off again, without a break. I think of those water carriers with their buckets strung on a pole across their shoulders, walking vast distances to bring back some precious liquid.

I arrived at a rest area. Evening had come so I stopped for the night.

There's a petrol station, playground, restaurant and a hotel: it's a large fully equipped service station! No need to unfold my tent; why bother – I took a room at the hotel instead. In the hallway, I met a man named René, a thin giant with close-cropped hair and a pinched mouth. He's been living here for ten years. He used to be homeless, lived on the streets. One day, whilst he was hanging around the service station near the hotel, a couple who were checking out offered him the key to their room:

"We don't need it anymore; make the most of

it. It's been paid for till tomorrow noon – it would be a pity not to use it."

The sheets were wrinkled and the towels were damp. But from that day onwards, René kept an eye out for people checking in and out of the hotel, paying special attention to couples with no luggage. He never slept on the streets again.

I showered and then I met René in the restaurant, where we dined together on instant soup and ice cream. He's become an expert in spotting 'passing couples'. He can tell them at a glance from thirty metres away!

"There are the loved up ones who walk in hand in hand, blatantly, a smile on their lips. These ones are so happy that on top of leaving you their key when checking out, they give you their voucher for a meal as well. Then there are the illicit ones, who meet in the car park guiltily before making their way to reception, touching each other furtively, looking anxiously around. They leave the hotel, embarrassed, running their fingers through their hair to smooth it down and then split up into two separate cars: 'I'll call you!'

There's the boss and the secretary: a timeless classic. The married couples wanting to spice things up and bring a little novelty into their lives. They organise everything, discuss it all beforehand: *'What do you think, dear?'* or sometimes they act on the spur of the moment, a sudden twist of the steering wheel and they end up in front of the hotel – *'Still young and crazy! Yeh!'*

They either come out smiling – *'We still love each other, after all!'* or disillusioned – *'That didn't change a thing.'* That's how it goes. There are the 'professionals', the lovers who stride in confidently, like regulars, inured to the thing. They say good bye with a peck on the cheek:

'See you again, some time?'

It's funny how easy it is to classify people, to sort one type from the other. It's become a game."

René was slurping up his soup loudly. He stopped to speak every so often, spoon in hand and then, mid-sentence, he'd plunge his cutlery back into his dish.

"I used to go over to them very politely, just as they were leaving. Some were worried they might get into trouble so they'd send me packing. Often, that meant things hadn't gone too well, back in the hotel room. It doesn't always work out. But among the various people – there are more than you'd think, believe me! – I always managed to find one happy couple who'd agree to it. The man would go back to reception and get me the key. I'd go in quietly – the people at the front desk knew me, and put up with it – in the end I stayed in every room in the hotel usually until noon the next day. Ah, I've seen it all… If you knew the goings on… Now, I have the hotel completely to myself.

I'm gonna heat up another packet, you want one? Summer vegetables, okay?"

As I lay on the bed in my room, I think of all those people passing through, who'd stayed here before me. Once the room's been cleaned and the bed's been made, it's as if there's nothing left of them. There may well be a hair caught in the weft of the carpet, or the clasp of an earring left under the bed, or a bit of nail concealed in a corner of the bathroom. For a thorough investigator, there'd be no lack of clues. But the place, although it's private for as long as you have it, it's intended to be impersonal, for the benefit of the general public, and their protection.

Of course, René knew a bit more about the occupants, seeing the rooms as he did before the cleaning lady. He lived in their wake, finishing their nights, breathing in their smells, using their sheets and towels. He was a keeper of secrets. Certain couples even entrusted him with their key out of a desire to show off – so that their secret coupling would be witnessed. He was a voyeur, appreciating the act of passion, from the more or less obvious traces they'd left behind. He became familiar with all sorts of post-coital stains and mess.

I notice there are several hand prints on the ceiling, as if someone had been walking on their hands, up there.

*

The 'noise' held sway throughout the world. No region escaped it; all the research to find a haven of peace and quiet was futile. From the depths of the Amazonian jungle to the Sahara's sweeping desert, from the summits of the Himalayas to the polar ice caps, from the smallest outpost to the most cosmopolitan mega-city, everywhere the sound was growing inexorably. They studied the so-called 'beings of silence' to try and unravel the mystery of their imperviousness. No reasonable explanation was ever found. Likewise, they carried out research to try and understand why the phenomenon was only affecting the human race. Animals as a whole didn't seem to be affected by the 'noise' and continued to live normally without any problems. Questions remained unanswered. And then the pain took over.

René has taken in two stray dogs; he's called them Löten and Ékely. They now roam around the hotel freely. He feeds them and they keep him company and let him stroke their heads. You can hear him calling them in the hallway:

"Löten! Ékely! Where are you? Dinner time!"

The two dogs then race down the stairs towards their adoptive master. René told me he's often seen stags, does and even wild boar wandering through the grounds or hanging about on the highway.

I hang *The Scream* on the wall facing the bed, in place of a faded pastoral in watercolours. It changes things. It's not quite the same room anymore; the atmosphere is less welcoming, less serene; the nights become a little more agitated, the experience more tormented. The only thing that's missing to complete the effect, is *The Vampire,* another of Munch's paintings. The average guest would probably be reluctant to stay here, fearing for their health. Personally, I'm okay with it. Stretched out naked on the bed, I expose myself fully to the figure, who is so shocked, he holds his head in his hands, and covers his ears instead of his eyes perhaps through a lack of coordination, shouting:

"Oh! Put that penis away, I don't want to know about it!"

I play around, imagining his prudishness.

I take a leisurely stroll around the grounds. It's a fairly large area next to the highway, equipped with all mod cons – a pretty convincing pocket of life. I can appreciate why you'd want to stay here, to make it home. If you hang around for a while, the complex starts to make perfect sense; it becomes a real place to stay in its own right, totally enjoyable, rather than simply an enforced stopover on the way to somewhere else. The places where we cross over, if you know how to spend time there, can be perfectly delightful. I remember the story of a man who arrived at an airport from an international flight, and never left again. He just stayed there, in the terminal, living with the comings and goings of the other passengers, for more than twenty years. He was very happy, in his island sanctuary, watching the waves of travellers rolling in to shore.

I also recollect the story of another man who'd chosen to live in an old people's home when he was thirty-five years old. If you think about it, a retirement home and a service area are quite similar. They're both full of restrooms, reminding us of our physical condition while at the same time extracting its essence. What delicious and fragile vulnerability! Our weakness is our strength; our smallness is our greatness. I smile in the face of death, the death that awaits me, and I love the life that pushes me towards it.

I browse the shelves of the shop at the petrol station. A lot of the items are out of date now; the sandwiches have gone mouldy in their wrapping; the cakes dried up in their packaging; the milk's gone off in all the rows of bottles. How much time has gone by? There are no obstacles to time anymore and so it flows freely. Days are no longer broken into hours or minutes, and extend indefinitely. My beard has grown without me noticing. I walk without moving. Where am I?

*

All along the highway, a wire fence prevents open access to the road as well as stopping people exiting without payment. But here and there, there are alternative routes in for the people who work there and for emergency vehicles. Every two kilometres there are telephones which connect to the emergency services. Besides that, a CCTV system covers all the essential places. Digital display panels inform motorists of any problems up ahead (accidents, breakdowns, objects on the road, stray animals etc.) or provide advice and information. A technician usually types out the different statements – no more than forty characters – and sends them to the display boards with just one click. *"It's 28°C today with risk of storms";* the message goes on, advising caution. A buzzard is perched on the display board, surveying the road. It's not in the least bothered by my being there. The creature looks down on me with an open beak.

Tramping along the highway is a bit like rowing across an ocean. Once, I ran out of petrol in the morning on the way to work – I thought I could make it. I pulled over onto the hard shoulder and set off for the nearest petrol station, five kilometres away, to buy a can of petrol. And suddenly I felt the full force of it, despite the short distance, the disproportion between the immensity of the highway and the paltry size of my own steps. Whilst I paddled along, dealing with the gust of the vehicles speeding past me, the road endlessly renewed itself before my eyes and I felt like I was following the horizon. That day, I discovered the strength of perseverance, the force of minimal effort, as I experienced the subtle virtues of walking. Running is ambitious and demands the active involvement of the entire body; walking is much more modest, requiring little of the muscles, so that the body becomes a vehicle for the spirit. It's a bit like riding a camel, perched on its back, swaying in motion with the animal's stride, the wind blowing in your hair, eyes fixed on the horizon.

I get a glimpse of a silhouette leaning on the railings of the bridge across the highway. As I get closer, I can make out a woman's shape. I stop at the bottom of the bridge and look up at her. She just stares at the highway, motionless, as if imitating the buzzard on the display board. You often see people standing on bridges, watching the road; you wonder what they're up to, whether they're going to jump or not; sometimes, they have a bike. I decide to pitch my tent near the bridge, on the grass and in the shade of a pillar.

Enora has lost a loved one, a child. His name was Tom and he was six years old. He drowned, was swept away by a river in flood. Enora blames herself, it's her fault, she couldn't hold onto him, couldn't save him. She's a nurse, she knows what it means to save a life. She'd like to put an end to it all, throw herself under the wheels of a truck. However, to start with, there are no trucks left, and then, she hesitates, she doesn't know anything anymore.

It reminds me of that story on the news, about a couple, who watched their two children die in similar circumstances, during torrential floods. The first one was carried away, swallowed up by the water, the other one, very young, died of cold in the arms of his father who was powerless to help him. A photo in the papers showed the man soaking wet in his underwear, having been pulled out of the water, looking crushed, his arms hanging useless, forever empty. The warmth of his body and all the love of a father weren't enough. His helpless guilt would never leave him.

Misfortune is an unavoidable part of life and there are always others worse off somewhere else in the world. But sometimes, an image, or a story, told often enough, becomes a heartbreaking symbol of human tragedy. There are many accounts of assorted disasters occurring all over the world, but few of these ever become a calamity of universal concern. It's not possible to revise Death, although in some cases it can seem almost bearable. But it can also be appalling, an absolute outrage. How then, do we keep from letting rip a scream of rage, of revolt, of despair, of love and hatred?

I put *The Scream* down against the pillar of the bridge. Wherever you put it, it always adds to the surroundings, with a sense of refinement and authority. It stands out like an apparition, a sign, a value. Most paintings can't withstand the loss of the space they hang in, and are simply overwhelmed by nature. However, *The Scream* can be displayed anywhere, with equal power. It strikes the mind's eye, never failing to stand out, regardless of the place it's shown. It never loses any of its strength and meaning. I understand the thieves: they had to get rid of it once they realised it's impossible to own it or to suppress or subdue it. Even inside its case, hidden in the boot of a car, it lived, it breathed. That's what's so disturbing about it.

Enora won't leave her post, her hands grip the railings, as she stares down at the void below. Having exhausted all possibilities, now she just feels numb. She's only a few metres away but I can't get any closer to her, without climbing the fence and then the bridge. Even then I'd need to approach her extremely carefully, like when you offer food to a starving person.

Any sudden movement and she might collapse on the spot. Better to keep her company from a safe distance, to try and create rapport. I don't have the soul of a Samaritan but I'm familiar with suffering. Mourning is an intimate affair, allowing no intrusion. Sympathy and kindness don't really help, and make you want to get away. Only an affable silence and an acceptance that there is nothing you can do, can help; the kind of silence that doesn't try to be too sensitive. A silence without an agenda; silent in the void, silent because there are no words. But a silence that's like a hand on the shoulder, modest, humble, human.

It's a beautiful day. I'm sitting on the grass, looking at the fields. The maize crops have withered and formed a rotting mulch from which wild shoots emerge. An abandoned tractor has lost its *raison d'être* and falls apart, piece by piece, with the grating sound of scrap metal. I look up at Enora. Clinging to her silence, she holds on with all her strength, the figurehead of a ghost ship on a childless sea. Life has gone; the survivors resemble the dead.

*

As I was crawling out of my tent this morning, I noticed Enora watching me, at first interested and then bemused. I let her watch me, without bothering too much. I just went about my usual morning routine; whistling casually while taking a piss in a ditch, jogging up and down the road, letting fly two or three right hooks. Then I did some stretching, reaching up to the sky with a loud: *Aaaaaagh!*

We could almost certainly love each other. I've always been lucky with unhappy women. They trust me. They pour out their hearts; open up; get involved. "You look harmless. A bit weird, but harmless," one actually confided. For a long time I've lived in a world full of feelings, of love and hate, good and bad, right and wrong, a world of cause and effect. And then, it all disappeared. All my certainties, all my beliefs slowly disintegrated to be replaced by a kind of fundamental vision of absolute fatalism. I wasn't living in the same world anymore. Everything stable around me collapsed like so many folding screens. I used to take an absurdist view so I could laugh at life. I loved to make wisecracks; as a rule, I never argued. I subscribed to the trend of gently letting myself go, with a slightly sickly smile on my lips. In daily life, I often came across as a bit of an outsider. Not mean, just "a bit weird, but harmless". The only danger lay in my detachment.

We could almost certainly love each other, Enora, with her dead child, and me... Perhaps, in another lifetime. Love requires naivety and innocence.

I lie down in the grass and watch the clouds passing across the most beautiful avenue in the world – there's one that looks like Eddie Mitchell, the curve looks like a kind of quiff. Enora feels increasingly silly and embarrassed, clinging on to the railings. She doesn't want to climb over it anymore, and would prefer to leave it be. But there's a guy, down there, who's starting to sing now:

"The girl with the sea green eyes...
And I couldn't take it anymore..."

– a right old din – that distracts her from her despair. She would never have jumped, but she would have been totally consumed by her grief to the point of madness. Instead, she has to endure the annoying presence of this stranger.

"Couldn't you be quiet or go somewhere else?"

Enora broke her silence as I was brushing the dust off some of my belongings. To get her out of her depressed state for good, I asked her to repeat herself:

"Sorry?"

"There's plenty of room elsewhere, why do

you have to camp right here, where I can see you?"

I acted all innocent and apologised. She was going to be okay now. She kept clinging on to the railings for a while, before finally letting go.

"You want some biscuits? When I throw you the packet... Catch it!"

She ate one. I started packing my bag. When I came out of the tent, there was no-one there. She'd disappeared; she was gone. Taking the packet of biscuits with her.

You see, that's how it is, there are people who watch the cars drive past, standing on the bridges over the roads and then, they carry on. Sometimes, they have a bike.

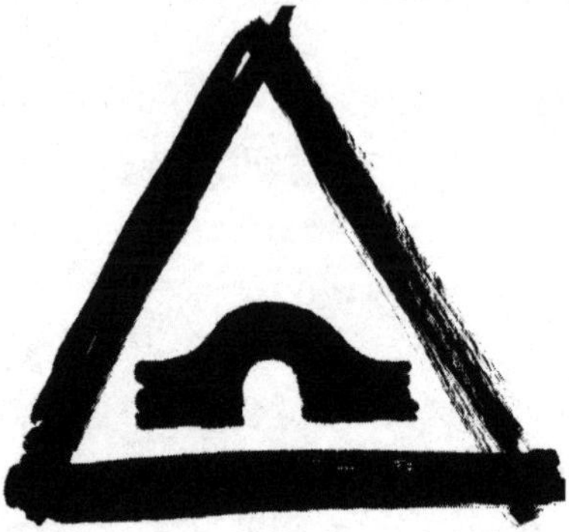

FIVE

I stride along the broken white lines that run down the highway like giant footprints, ten strides for me to one for him. I've lost the carrying case for *The Scream*, I don't know where.

When I reached one of those digital display boards (*Today it's 18°C*) I intended to hang Munch's masterpiece from it, as if from a gallows. I'd rifled through several car boots earlier, looking for something I could tie it up with. I unwrapped *The Scream* and hoisted it over the roadway. I tied off the end of the rope round the safety barrier and stepped back to contemplate the picture. It was gently swinging in the breeze, attached by a noose to the display board. It came to rest three or four metres off the ground, at a slight angle, like a portent, a highway effigy. I stood there for a while to admire my installation. But when I looked for *The Scream*'s case to put it away, I couldn't find it anywhere. I set off again, carrying the painting under my arm, like an art student.

An ambulance surged up behind me, its siren blaring. I had to jump aside quickly to get out of its way. It carried on at high speed and disappeared, destroying the silence with its terrible howl.

*

The very first victims of the 'noise' were taken to hospital, where they were given a placebo in place of a sedative. The emergency wards were inundated with groups of moaning people, all holding their heads in both hands. Doctors and nurses weren't able to cope with this and hospitals soon saw desperate scenes where suicides, murders and riots all took place. Some people dragged themselves in agony through the corridors, in search of a release, of some kind of cure. Then people stopped going to the hospital altogether. They died alone, in a corner, in a

THE SCREAM

recess, sat up against a wall, on the floor of the bathroom, curled up on their beds, gripping onto trees, or in their car on the roadside, hunched up in pain.

*

The broken white lines stop suddenly. The hard shoulders on both sides of the road have ended too. The only thing left to mark the way is the central crash barrier. The road surface seems rougher and more uneven, making me trip and scuff the soles of my shoes. I'm starting to stumble, panic. Up until now, I've been walking automatically, delighting in the forward motion of my steps. Feelings of fragility, of being weak and frightened come upon me. It's like a dreadful far away thought slowly taking shape, a truth that's gradually revealed, a premonition that grows stronger and stronger. The road is definitely taking me somewhere – I know that now – and I'm getting closer.

The highway passes over a small hill then sharply turns into a secondary road. There's a sudden narrowing, and it goes down from four lanes to two. The crash barrier separating the traffic comes to a sudden end. The wire fence along the side of the road stops abruptly in the middle of a field. A road sign indicates that the speed limit is restricted to ninety kilometres per hour. Then the highway vanishes and gives way to a small country road like a tender shoot.

I recognise this small road right away. A little further on, there's a second sign, a yellow one, that warns drivers about the risks of gravel to windscreens. The road has just been resurfaced – hence the absence of any markings. As it had been a particularly harsh winter road surfaces had been badly damaged. Once the weather improved, the maintenance work had begun to repair the holes.

*

The road ran across a vast, hilly terrain where fields stretched as far as the eye could see. Usually there was a strong wind that made it hard going for cyclists caught short of breath. It seemed endless to us, this road. It had been snowing all through January and snow had built up on the verges, causing several vehicles to get stuck, bogged down under heaps of snow. We'd just moved in. The house was nothing special – apart from the price – a small detached house painted beige, ideal for a 'young couple starting out'. The village was a bit isolated, a long way from the shops, four hundred souls in the middle of nowhere, plus two – soon to be three.

We used to go for walks in the village and on the paths all around it. The tractors made deep furrows in the ground with their big wheels. The birth was due at the beginning of May. Whilst out walking, she'd hold her belly with both hands, like a little bag of cement where life had taken shape. I'd put my arm around her shoulder, protectively. We lived in a quiet and predictable linear little world, safe and sure of our tomorrow. There were no real problems, except for some big dark cloud in the sky that might shorten one of our walks: "We forgot the umbrella". Our petty worries usually came to nothing. And the child would enhance our happy, untroubled existence.

Drivers thought it was okay to speed on this long straight road, despite its ups and downs. The vastness of the surrounding countryside, the wide-open spaces, only increased their craving for speed and mastery. Yet, accidents were rare. I once walked past one; two cars had crashed head-on in the dip between two hills. These dips threw up all sorts of risks, for the cyclist to the tractor to tiny unlicensed electric cars, which were unusually common in the area – possibly a local trend. The crash must have been extremely bad; both cars were unrecognisable. The road always looked absolutely interminable: people wanted to get to the end of it as fast as possible.

I've often travelled across this region, in one direction or another. A little further on, there's an adjoining road which leads to Montapeine, a hamlet off to the right. A lane leading down from a farm runs opposite to this, forming a kind of crossroads. I'm almost there. I'll be there soon, once I get over these two hills, one after the other like the humps of a camel. They make the heart race. I'm getting closer.

The countryside is deserted, no sign of an abandoned car or a stray animal. The sky suddenly grows overcast; the wind forms streaks of glowing red clouds like blood streaming down a windscreen. I carry on walking; my mouth twists into a fixed grin. In front of me there's a light swirling around. Winter is very nearly over, we're only seventy-two hours away from Spring. A glimmer of light, the last flicker of a fleeting heart. There's a flashing light attached to an extendable pole which rises above the road like a lantern. What it signals is still out of sight, concealed by the hilly terrain; there's not much time for the imagination to take in the coming scene.

I see her face, her eyes look at me; I hear her voice talking to me; we lived in a small village in the countryside; we were expecting a child; I see a tractor stood on the verge, further on, a red car in the ditch; I see flashing lights, people busy working and others standing by, watching.

On top of the little hill, the vista opens out. I stand still, my bag slung over my shoulder and Edvard Munch's painting tucked under my arm. The flashing light which is attached to a tripod and runs off a battery, has been set up about fifty metres uphill from the accident. I can see two police cars, a fire-engine and an ambulance. The tractor has come to rest on the right side of the road, without any visible damage. Another car, a grey one, is parked on the hard shoulder and its owner is talking with a police constable who is making notes for a statement. Two hitch-hikers, a girl and a boy with rucksacks, stand there watching. The police report doesn't mention them as witnesses; they were probably just passing by, probably on their way to the main road, a few kilometres away.

I put down my bag and propped up *The Scream* at the foot of the flashing light, as if to add sound to the luminous beacon. I go closer. People are speaking all around in low tones, out of respect for the seriousness of the accident. The ambulance is parked next to the red car planted in the ditch. Paramedics lean over a stretcher with deft movements. The police have stopped the traffic and ask the drivers waiting at the scene to please turn around and go another way. Suddenly, I hear a song by Florent Pagny escaping at full volume from an open car window. The driver turns around and leaves. The music fades away before vanishing completely.

I go closer. I pass the police man questioning the owner of the second car. In the witness statement, the driver, a nurse who was on her way to work, says that she was some way behind the victim's car. She didn't actually see the collision. However, she heard it distinctly and then she came across the red car stuck in the ditch. She stopped immediately.

The driver of the tractor, a tall, thin man with a surly face, remains alone by his machine, with his arms crossed, watching the paramedics. Two dogs wait in the tractor behind the windows, panting. In his statement, the farmer explains that he went down the lane from the farm and stopped with his hazard warning lights flashing. He turned into the road as usual and then felt a sudden shock at the back of his trailer. He came to a halt. The nurse, who had got out of her car, and the farmer both ended up next to the damaged vehicle at the same time. The woman declares that "the victim was unconscious and in a really bad state" – a worrying thing to hear coming from a nurse.

I inch forward, reluctantly; the truth is I'm barely moving. I feel like I'm sinking in quicksand. I reach the ambulance, its doors are open; they're waiting to load the stretcher. But, the paramedics are still busy with the victim. The two firemen chat in low tones, well-used to dealing with such events. As I pass by I hear one of them talking about some couscous he had in a restaurant at Château-Rémy last night, "absolutely divine"; he and his wife had really enjoyed themselves. The other one nods: "That's good to know." A few metres away, the doctors are checking for any signs of life.

They decide to take the victim to the hospital. Suddenly, everybody gets moving, the stretcher is loaded into the ambulance. A convoy begins to form. The sirens wail.

*

I sit in Accident & Emergency on an orange plastic chair, a bit like the ones you find in a métro station. I no longer have either my bag or the painting by Edvard Munch. How long have I been here? At the front desk, the receptionist is tapping away at the computer keyboard behind the counter. Occasionally, she raises her head and glances in my direction. I wait. They'll call me.

A doctor will come.

"Sir? – Yes… What is it?"

A few seats away, on my right, a woman anxiously waits for news, clenching her fists.

"Excuse me, I don't have any change on me; I left my handbag in the car and I'm parked quite far away from here. Could you lend me one euro for a coffee, please?"

Usually, when people ask me for something, some money, a signature on a petition or even simply my opinion, I say 'no' right away, without even bothering to listen; I admit this is partly pure laziness but mainly, I'm just pig-headed. This time, I make an exception. I fish in my pocket and pass her a coin. She goes over to reception:

"I'm going for a coffee, I'll be right back".

When she reappears, barely two minutes later, she asks:

"Any news yet?"

The sight of her face won't leave me. Right now she's on the operating table, somewhere at the end of a corridor, and people are trying to keep the life inside her from leaving. Her body is suffering and bleeding. The doctor – "Follow me, please" – will say there was nothing they could do; they were giving her blood but it wasn't enough. I'll casually notice the doctor looks a bit like a popular singer, slightly retro, an old crooner, with his good cheek bones and sympathetic eyes. There's a badge pinned to his shirt: *Doctor Daniel Meyer*. The list of injuries he'll describe to me in his office will be distressing.

"You understand, in these circumstances, nothing could be done for the baby either; he was already gone."

Death was dwelling inside her. He'll announce the time of death, with a bewildering and disturbing accuracy. My eyes will unconsciously fix on a cast iron radiator:

"Can I see her?

I'm waiting again, on another orange plastic chair, for someone to come and find me; I'm waiting for it all to be over. They are preparing her, cleaning her, fixing her up. Her personal effects, watch, jewellery, purse, will be handed back to me at the police station. They'd been taken away earlier, at the scene of the accident. The woman next to me, losing patience, is clenching her fists so tight, she might crush her hands. Eventually, she goes to get her bag from her car. She wants to return the money I gave her.

All of a sudden, I feel the need to say it, to pronounce the words, to tell someone she's dead, DEAD. There's a payphone in the hallway of the Accident & Emergency unit. I only have one person to call: the friend. When the phone rings, he's working on a new model boat, a twin-masted sailing ship for his miniature collection. There are things that you'd never thought you'd ever have to say, because they don't make any sense, because they're too absurd, too unbelievable:

"M. is dead."

But they don't believe it.

"Stop it, what are you talking about?"

To keep it short, you sum up the situation, back up the facts. Then you hang up. That's it, now it's been said. But you need to say it again, to repeat it. To repeat it over and over, again and again. Louder and louder.

I sit back on my seat, drained, wiped out.

The phone rings at the reception desk and the girl answers it.

"Sir! You can go up to the second floor now. They're waiting for you."

The woman next to me watches, shakily, as I stand up. I take the lift to the second floor. Two women in green gowns come over to me.

"Are you going to be all right? She's over there."

The room is small, very bright. She's lying on a hospital bed on wheels; a sheet is pulled up to the shoulders. Her eyes are closed. I stand back.

I opened my mouth. At the same time, I raised my hands. My eyes opened wide. I gripped my head in both hands, covering my ears firmly. Then I started screaming, like an explosion, a big-bang, the crash of a meteor, the smash of a tidal wave. I screamed, screamed my heart out...

...and the whole universe reverberated with my scream, a scream of love, of hate, of life, of death.

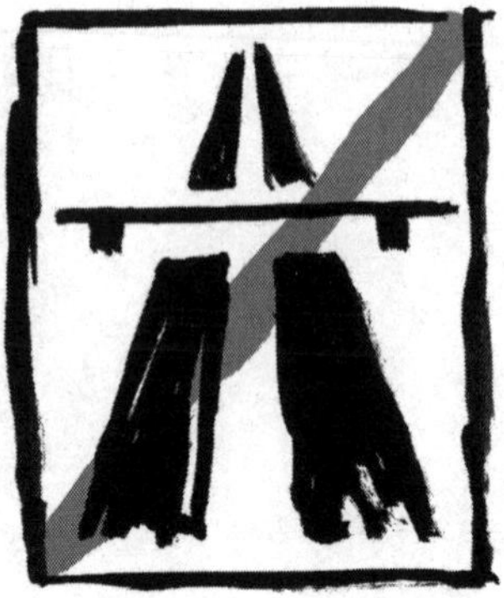

If you enjoyed *The Scream*, why not try:

POMEGRANATE SKY
Louise Soraya Black

Winner of The Virginia Prize For Fiction 2009

Living in post-revolutionary Tehran, Layla refuses to bow to the ayatollah's rules, resisting her mother's relentless attempts to find her a suitable husband. Instead, she embarks on an illicit affair with her art teacher Keyvan, and they tentatively imagine a future together.

But the sudden death of her uncle, an outspoken journalist, raises many unanswered questions and when Layla's cousin, who is visiting from America, is arrested by the morality police, the Komiteh, Layla's plans for the future begin to unravel.

Beneath the polished surface of upper-class Iranian life lies pain, fear and dark, dark secrets.

'a bittersweet tale of betrayed trust and ruptured innocence... the feel for colour and language is vibrant'
The Guardian first novel choice

'Vividly written, fresh and eloquent, a girl's poignant tale of love and menace in contemporary Iran.'
Fay Weldon

£8.99
ISBN 9781906582104

MOSAIC DECEPTIONS
Patrick Gooch

When Matt Clements meets an enigmatic prophet on the Kurdistan border, he is set on the trail of ancient relics that have profound consequences for our time. Assembling his team, he travels to the most remote desert regions of the Middle East, unaware that the search for evidence endangers all their lives.

In a race against time, Matt must outwit his adversaries to present his discoveries publicly in New York – discoveries that will send shockwaves throughout the Western world and rewrite history as we know it.

'Thought provoking and intelligent thriller' *Metro*

'…A real page-turner that jolts us out of complacency with a bold and clever plot…' *Dazed & Confused*

£8.99
ISBN 9781906582142

Coming soon…

KIPLING & TRIX

Mary Hamer

Winner of the Virginia Prize for Fiction

As small children, Rudyard Kipling and his sister Trix lived an enchanted life in India playing with their beloved servants and running around freely. Their happiness came to an abrupt end when they were sent back to England to live with strangers and forced to conform to the strict rules of Edwardian society in an alien country.

Both brother and sister grew up to become writers, although one lived in the shadow of the other's genius. Rudyard Kipling's incredible life is known to many while his poetry and books have been read by millions – but what became of his talented younger sister? Trix's story, full of love and lies, became a distressing family secret that was hidden from the world...

Mary Hamer has unearthed the truth about Trix. In this fictionalised account of their lives, the author goes to the heart of the relationship between a difficult brother and his troubled sister and explores how their early lives shaped the very different people they were later to become.

£9.99
ISBN: 9781906582340

DAFNE & THE DOVE

Jonathan Falla

When Silke Khan and her husband Theo come crashing into Dr Mattieu Macanan's carefully constructed life as a medic in the Patagonian jungle, his world is irrevocably altered...

An avid pilot, Theo wishes to run an airmail service to the area, one of the remotest parts of South America, and Mattieu must face intrusion and change. But what has he been hiding from? Should his way of life - and that of the local tribe he seeks to protect - be preserved at any cost?

A beautifully written and absorbing story of colonialism and repressed desire, exploring the human psyche from a remote part of Chile around 1915...

Reviews of Falla's previous work:

'A book saturated with loving detail, unpredictable and opulent.' *The Sunday Times*

'Refreshing, unapologetically subjective and original.' *The New Statesman*

£8.99
ISBN: 9781906582388

www.aurorametro.com